*W*herever Amelia went she was followed by her trusty pack of wolves. As rain hit the window she ran down the stairs towards her bright pink wellington boots, shortly followed by three big fluffy hounds.
Dressed for a wet and muddy walk they weren't letting a little bad weather dampen their spirits. 'Why stay indoors when there's still so much fun to be had outside?' Amelia thought to herself.

What I Love About You

Written and illustrated by Ellie Adkinson
For 'Life With Malamutes'

Their regal house cat Milo glared through the window disapprovingly as Mum and Dad gathered Amelia and her snow dogs into the car. Teddy and Niko started to howl with excitement, their confident singing echoing down the street much to their neighbours dismay.

The third pup Phil sat down next to Amelia to rest his head against her shoulder. Unlike the others his voice was soft and he always had a certain shyness about him.

They pulled up to their favourite park and one by one they hopped out of the car, straight onto the soggy field around them. Amelia giggled as her wellies sank into the wet grass and the excited dogs ran around her in circles ready to play. Phil dived into the nearest muddy puddle and shook his golden coat all over his family. "You're very happy all of a sudden" Dad laughed as he wiped the raindrops from his jacket.

As they made their way down a path surrounded by the tallest trees Teddy and Niko ran ahead to investigate, leaving a nervous Phil to wonder what was in the distance. Phil was unique and wasn't like other dogs. His beautiful fur had always shed faster and he constantly thought about how it made him look to others. He held back for a moment to look at a patch on his body where hair was missing. There was less there than yesterday.

*W*hat if they were to run into other dogs that day? Thoughts ran through Phil's mind as he slowly began to catch up. As they continued along the wooded path it wasn't long before the sound of endless panting came rushing towards them. Out of the bushes came two lively Dalmatian dogs, all they wanted to do was play with their new found friends. "This way! Follow us!" One barked as Teddy and Niko darted after them to find mischief up ahead.

Four dogs chased each other round and round as Mum and Dad chatted away with the family who had brought their Dalmatians. Phil desperately wanted to join in by exploring every inch of the forest around him but something made him walk in the opposite direction. As he wandered over to a large puddle he looked down at his reflection and started to sigh. Knowing she needed to be by his side, Amelia followed and looked into the water with him.

"What's wrong?" Amelia asked as Phil lifted his head to look at everyone enjoying their day. He looked back down at parts of his body and Amelia knew she needed to help. "They're really cute dogs" she beamed. "But they're not as special as you are". She hopped from one puddle to the next, laughing and asking Phil to join her. Within minutes he had forgotten why he was down and slowly began to show the side of him he had tried to hide.

Phil was covered in mud from head to tail and he was finally enjoying his day out. As everyone else wondered why he wasn't playing with them, something amazing started to happen. The Dalmatians had ventured over with a young boy who had been watching them play and wanted to say hello. He ran towards Phil as fast as his little legs could carry him and gave him the biggest hug.

"*I* wish my doggies had such a fluffy coat!" The boy cried with excitement. Phil couldn't believe what was happening! "Where are all these compliments coming from?" he thought to himself. His family always tried to make him feel better and now he really wanted to believe it. With his new found confidence he started to howl and bounded towards the rest of his family and friends.

As if by magic Phil had started becoming the dog he was always meant to be. He was beginning to feel like he was part of the pack even though he looked and sounded different. As the hours passed and the rain began to ease off it was time to say goodbye to those who had made a bigger impact on him than they realised. Phil and his family waved as two tired Dalmatians and their humans walked off into the distance.

The car journey home was a lot brighter than it was that morning. The sun was beginning to set and as they all made their way through the front door, tails began to wag as it was fast approaching dinner time. Muddy paw prints covered the kitchen as all three dogs scrambled towards their bowls. "I think it's time for a bath" Mum broke the news as she looked towards Phil. As much as he enjoyed playing in water, Phil did not enjoy bath time.

MILO

PHIL

Soapy water filled the bath tub and Phil's nerves started to come back as he slowly dipped one paw to see if it was warm. Mum stood waiting with a towel as Teddy and Niko jumped right in, splashing the walls and Phil as they went. Amelia picked up one of their toys and placed it on the water to let it float. "You have to save your toy from the waves!" she played along to try and help. This was a test of Phil's new bravery. His pack made some space for him to climb into the bath, his legs were shaking as he finally climbed into the bubbles.

"*I* did it!" Phil had amazed himself and everyone in the room! Even a relaxed cat like Milo couldn't believe it! "I'm so proud of you" Mum told him as she reached for some shampoo that was made just for his special golden coat. That evening they would all sit on the couch by the fire to warm themselves after a long stormy day. As Amelia slowly closed her eyes and went to sleep on Phil's back, he smiled to himself as he felt content. For that was the day he finally realised just how beautiful and unique he really was. And he couldn't have done it without Amelia by his side.

To Amelia, may you never forget your furry friends that guided your path, taught you to love, compassion and never to judge a book by its cover. Be strong, be bold and be you. We are proud of the little girl you are today and the woman you'll become. When the pages of our book end, you'll be the best chapter.

With love from Mummy and Daddy

CPSIA information can be obtained
at www.ICGtesting.com
Printed in the USA
LVHW071646221122
733801LV00012B/628